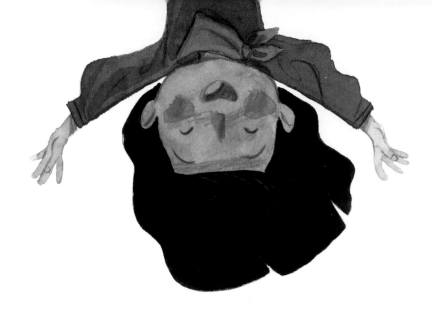

STERLING CHILDREN'S BOOKS
New York

An Imprint of Sterling Publishing Co., Inc.
1166 Avenue of the Americas
New York, NY 10036

ISBN 978-1-4549-2034-2

Distributed in Canada by Sterling Publishing Co., Inc.
c/o Canadian Manda Group, 664 Annette Street
Toronto, Ontario, Canada M6S 2C8
Distributed in the United Kingdom by GMC Distribution Services
Castle Place, 166 High Street, Lewes, East Sussex, England BN7 1XU
Distributed in Australia by NewSouth Books
45 Beach Street, Coogee, NSW 2034, Australia

For information about custom editions, special sales, and premium and corporate purchases, please contact Sterling Special Sales at 800-805-5489 or specialsales@sterlingpublishing.com.

Manufactured in China

Lot #:
2 4 6 8 10 9 7 5 3 1
07/17

www.sterlingpublishing.com

The artwork for this book was created using watercolor and colored pencil.
Design by Irene Vandervoort

Famously Phoebe

BY Lori Alexander

ILLUSTRATED BY Aurélie Blard-Quintard

STERLING CHILDREN'S BOOKS
New York

This is Phoebe.

And this is Phoebe's family.

Click!

No matter what Phoebe did, no matter where Phoebe went, she was always surrounded by . . .

Clickity! Click!

The cameras had been there as long as she could remember.

Nothing could stop them.

Phoebe's face was *everywhere.*

which led her to believe one thing—

She must be famous!
Being famous meant lots of special attention
at the grocery store, the bank,

or just plain walking
down the street.

Of course, Phoebe preferred traveling first-class.

Even so, Phoebe never missed a chance to
give back to her fans.
She loved them as much as they loved her.

Oh, there were a *few*

problems with the fame.

Privacy was an issue.

And the fashion critics
were ruthless.

But overall, life in the spotlight was spectacular.
Until . . .

. . . a younger co-star arrived on-set.

Her name was Rose. And even though she was
teeny-weeny, she hogged all the spotlight.

This was not in Phoebe's contract.
She complained to the producers.

When that didn't work, she tried to dazzle them
with song and dance.

But for the first time, no one was watching.
They were too busy fussing over the new girl.

Rose only liked **one** kind of toy.

Rose only drank **one** kind of milk.

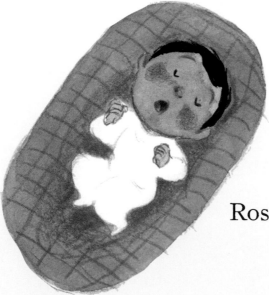

Rose only slept **one** kind of way.

Geesh, thought Phoebe. **What a diva!**

Phoebe wasn't famous anymore.

No more first-class travel. No more packed performances.

No more special attention.

Phoebe felt like an extra—
or worse yet, a personal assistant.

The worst part? Rose didn't even want to be famous.
At her first photo shoot, all she did was wail.

Not a single set,

not a perfectly placed prop

could get Rose to smile.

The crew grew desperate.

That's when Phoebe saw her big break.

She took the stage! She stole the spotlight!

She gave her audience action and adventure.

Drama.

And lots of comedy.

A hush came over the crowd.
That's when Phoebe noticed—

Rose was smiling!

Phoebe gave an encore performance.
And out came Rose's very first laugh.

From then on,
Phoebe didn't worry
so much about being
famous.

She landed a new
role: Big Sister.
It turned out that she was
born to play the lead.

Being a big sister meant
trips to the spa,

fancy dinners,
and evenings at
the theater.

Now, more than anything, she loved her private time.
Just Phoebe and Rose . . .

. . . and all the other stars.